The EMPEROR'S NEW CLOTHES

by
Hans Christian Andersen

Illustrated by
Pamela Baldwin Ford

Troll Associates

Troll Associates, Mahwah, N.J.

Library of Congress Catalog Card Number: 78-18063
ISBN 0-89375-132-4

A long, long time ago, there lived an Emperor who was very fond of clothes. He spent all his money on new clothes, and he had a different outfit for every hour of the day. He did not care about anything else in the world except clothes. While other kings and emperors spent their time in their council chambers, this Emperor spent his time in his dressing room.

One day, two rogues arrived in the busy town where the Emperor lived. They said they were weavers, but they were really thieves. "We can weave the most unusual cloth in the world," they said. "It is invisible to anyone who is not fit for his office, or who is impossibly stupid!"

When the Emperor heard about the remarkable fabric, he thought, "I must have some of it. With a suit made of this special cloth, I can find out who is smart and who is stupid. And I can tell if anyone is unfit for his job!"

So he sent for the weavers, and paid them a large sum of
money to weave their wonderful cloth.

The rogues called for the finest silk and for thread
made of pure gold. Then they set up two weaving looms,
and pretended to work. But the looms remained empty,
for the scoundrels had hidden the silk and gold!

After a while, the Emperor wondered how the weavers were coming along. He decided to send his honored old minister to examine the cloth and report

back to him. "He will be able to see the fabric, for he is
certainly not stupid. And no one could be better suited to
his job than he is."

But when the old minister saw the empty looms, he thought, "Good heavens! I can't see a thing!" Of course, he did not say this out loud. Then the rogues asked him to come and examine the cloth closely. They pointed out the beautiful pattern, and commented on the lovely colors. The old minister rubbed his eyes and looked again, but still he saw nothing. "Am I a fool?" he wondered. "Could it be that I am unfit for my high office? I certainly can't see any cloth!"

"Well, what do you think of it?" asked one of the rogues.

"Oh, it is splendid!" replied the old minister. As the rogues talked about the color, pattern, and texture of the cloth, the old minister listened carefully to everything they said. When he returned to the Emperor, he was able to tell him exactly what the cloth looked like.

Before long, the two rogues called for more fine silk and more gold thread. But when it was brought to them, they hid it, and went on working at the empty looms.

Soon the Emperor sent another official of the court to find out how the fabric was coming, and when it would be finished. But no matter how hard he blinked and rubbed his eyes, the court official could see nothing on the empty loom.

"I am not stupid," he said to himself, "so I must be unfit for my job. But no one will ever know it, for I will pretend that I can see the fabric." And so he went back to the Emperor and said, "It is the most beautiful cloth I have ever seen!"

By now, the whole town was talking about the remarkable weavers and their unusual cloth. Everyone wanted to see how stupid and useless his neighbor was. The Emperor found that he could wait no longer to see

the fabric himself. So he called the most trusted members
of his court together—including the two who had already
seen the cloth. And they all went to the room where the
two rogues were busily working at their looms.

As soon as they entered the room, the old minister said, "There! Didn't I say it was beautiful?"

"And look at the lovely pattern!" remarked the other court official. All the other officials nodded wisely and agreed. Of course, they could not see anything on the looms, but they thought everyone else *could.*

At first, the Emperor just stared. "What is this?" he thought. "I don't see a thing! But that means I am either

impossibly stupid or unfit to be Emperor. How distress-
ing!" But then he said, out loud, "This fabric is truly
magnificent!" And he looked ever so closely at the
imaginary cloth and added, "It is the finest and most
beautiful cloth I have ever seen!"

Then all the people in the room looked, and stared,
and gazed at the empty looms, and everyone agreed that
the cloth was beautiful.

"Outstanding," all the officials cried, looking at the empty looms. "Delightful! Superb!"

The Emperor gave the two rogues the title "Official Court Weavers." He told them to begin cutting the material at once, and to make it into a beautiful suit of clothes for him. He would wear the outfit in a great procession through the streets of the town.

All night long, the two rogues stayed awake and pretended to cut and sew the cloth. Their scissors and their needles without thread flashed in the candlelight. And in the morning they said, "The Emperor's new clothes are finished."

When the Emperor came to see his new outfit, the rogues held up an imaginary coat and pair of pants and said, "Here are your jacket and trousers, Your Highness." And then they held up a long robe that was not there, and said, "Feel how light each garment is. When you wear these clothes, you might even think you have nothing on at all!"

At once, the Emperor removed all his old clothes, and began dressing in his remarkable new outfit. The rogues assisted him, pretending to tie this, and fasten that, and button something else. Finally, the Emperor stood before the mirror and admired himself.

"Everything fits perfectly," announced the rogues.
"And indeed, Your Majesty looks marvelous!"

The Emperor turned and said, "Then let the procession begin!" Two of the court attendants bent down and picked up the ends of the long train which they could not see. But they said nothing, for they did not want to be called stupid fools. Then they followed the Emperor, holding their hands high, to keep the train of the imaginary robe off the ground.

As the Emperor and his procession walked through the streets of the town, people leaned out their windows to watch. And since they did not want their neighbors to

think they were stupid or unfit for their jobs, they said things like, "How lovely the Emperor's new clothes are!" and "Isn't that a magnificent suit of clothes!"

Suddenly one of the children said, "But he hasn't any clothes on!" And of course, the child was right. Then the townspeople saw how foolish they had been.

Soon everyone was whispering, "He isn't wearing any clothes—the Emperor has nothing on!"

At last the Emperor realized that it was true. A wise and honest child had shown them all the truth. But he said, "Let the procession continue!" His attendants continued to hold up the invisible train, and the Emperor held his head up high. There was nothing else to be done!